This is the story of Gingerbread Fred.

You can read it in a chair, or read it in bed,

You can get someone else to read it instead!

There's something else. Can you guess what?

On every page there's a mouse to spot!

Gingerbread Fred

Nick and Claire Page

Illustrations by Sara Baker

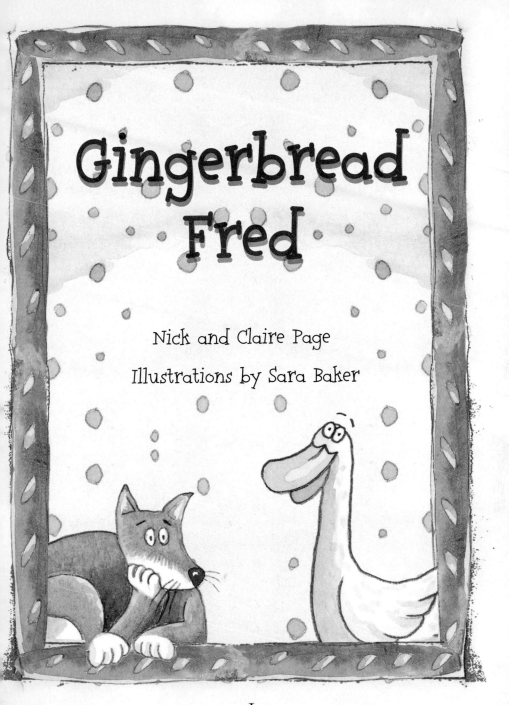

make
believe
ideas

There once was a little old baker
And a little old baker's wife,
One day they baked a gingerbread man
Who magically came to life!

The name that they gave him was
Gingerbread Fred.
And they said: "Don't go out on the street!
You are not a real boy, you're a biscuit –
And that makes you yummy to eat!"

But before you could say
"JAMMY DOUGHNUTS!"
Their gingerbread son
Started to run!

And Gingerbread Fred said...

"Run, run, run,
As fast as you can.
You can't catch me,
I'm the gingerbread man!"

First, Gingerbread Fred reached a garden,
Where a cat lay asleep in the flowers.
"Oh MEE-WOW!" said cat.
"Here comes breakfast!
I've been waiting for hours and hours!"

But before you could say
"CHELSEA BUNS!"
Fred didn't wait –
He started to skate!

And Gingerbread Fred said...

"Skate, skate, skate,
As fast as you can.
You can't catch me,
I'm the gingerbread man!"

Next, Gingerbread Fred reached a farmyard,
Where a dog lay asleep in the hay,
"Oh BOW-WOW!" said the dog.
"Must be lunchtime!
It's a gingerbread man takeaway!"

But before you could say
"LEMON CHEESECAKE!"
Fred turned aside
And started to ride!

And Gingerbread Fred said...

"Ride, ride, ride,
As fast as you can.
You can't catch me,
I'm the gingerbread man!"

Then Gingerbread Fred reached the river,
Where a fox sat, just watching the fish.
"Need some help?" said the fox.
"Just jump on my back.
I can take you across, if you wish."

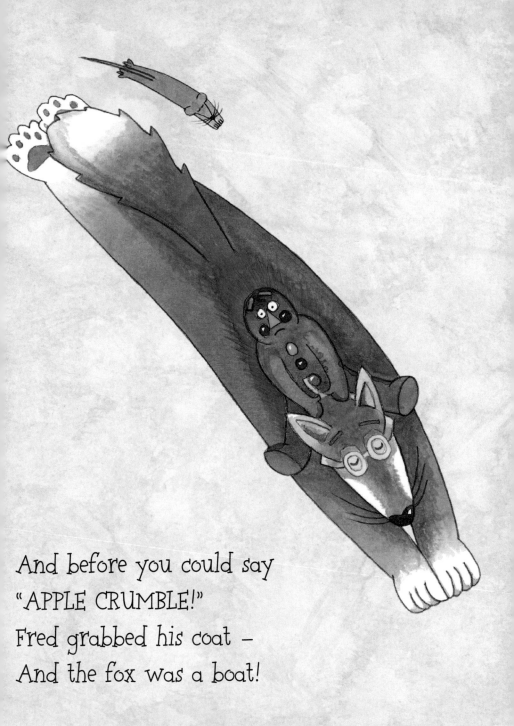

And before you could say
"APPLE CRUMBLE!"
Fred grabbed his coat –
And the fox was a boat!

And Gingerbread Fred said...

"Swim, swim, swim,
As fast as you can.
You can't catch me,
I'm the gingerbread man!"

The fox said to Fred:
"Move up further,"
As the water steadily rose.
"Don't get wet!" said the fox.
"You'll go soggy,
It's best if you sit on my nose."

Quite soon, they were over the river,
And Gingerbread Fred said: "Goodbye!"
"Not so fast," said the fox.
"There's one more thing;
Now, how would you like to fly?"

And before you could say
"GINGER SNAPS!"
Fred was thrown high –
Right up in the sky!

And Gingerbread Fred said...

24

"Fly fly, fly,
As fast as you can,
You can't catch me,
I'm the..."

CRUNCH! SCRUNCH! MUNCH!
The fox had him for lunch.

And Gingerbread Fred said...
Nothing.
(Ever again.)

Ready to tell

Oh no! Some of the pictures from this story have been mixed up! Can you retell the story and point to each picture in the correct order?

Picture dictionary

Encourage your child to read these harder words from the story and gradually develop their basic vocabulary.

baker

breakfast

fish

gingerbread man

ride

river

run

skate

wife

Key words

Here are some key words used in context.
Help your child to use other words
from the border in simple sentences.

There **was** a little old baker.

They baked **a** gingerbread man.

"Fly as fast as you **can.**"

The **dog** saw Gingerbread Fred.

"**Get** on my back."

Bake Gingerbread Fred

Ask a grown-up to help you bake Fred and his friends.
You can eat them if they look like they're running away!

You will need

100 g butter • 3 tbsp golden syrup • 350 g self-raising
flour • ready-made icing in a tube • 1-2 tsp ground
ginger • 100 g caster sugar • 1 egg, beaten • saucepan
• mixing bowl • large spoon • lightly greased baking
sheet • gingerbread man cutter • chocolate beans

What to do

1 Turn the oven on to 180°C / 350°F / gas mark 4.
2 Melt the butter and syrup in the pan over a gentle heat.
3 Put the flour, ginger and sugar in a mixing bowl.
Add the melted butter and syrup, stir in slightly and
then add the egg.
4 Mix the ingredients together until smooth and then
leave for 15 minutes to cool.
5 Roll out to a thickness of 6mm and use the cutter
to cut out the Gingerbread Fred shapes.
6 Place on a the baking sheet and cook in the middle
of the oven for about eight minutes, or until golden
brown. Remove and leave to cool.
7 Use icing to make the eyes and mouth, and use
chocolate beans stuck on with a spot of icing for buttons.